ALEX CROFT

MISSING!

Collins

LONDON AND GLASGOW

First published 1967

PRINTED AND MADE IN GREAT BRITAIN BY
WM. COLLINS SONS AND CO. LTD.
LONDON AND GLASGOW

CONTENTS

1. Graveyard of tanks

TAFFY MORRIS came slowly back to consciousness with the feeling that someone had got his head on an anvil and was thumping it with a hammer. To make matters worse someone began to sing. The little Welshman liked singing, but the mournful voice droning away quite close to him only made his throbbing headache seem worse. He wanted to tell the singer to shut up, but was too weak to do anything but screw up his eyes even more, and hope that the hammer banging away at his head would soon stop.

The singer stopped, then began again, his voice deep and mournful:

" All alone—I'm so all alone
There is no one else, but you.
All alone, by the telephone,
Waiting for—a ring—a ting—a—ling,
I'm all alone, every evening
All alone, feeling blue;
Wondering where you are,
And how you are

And if you are
All alone—too!"

Taffy nodded, without opening his eyes.
He felt like that. He wanted to be all alone.
If a telephone bell had jingled nearby he
would have screamed in protest. His head
felt as if it would burst. Then, without
warning, the singer began again:

"All alone, I'm so all alone—there is no
one else but you."

"Oh, for pete's sake, stop!" Taffy
pleaded, and opened his eyes. The singing
did stop and Taffy heard a swift, hissing
intake of breath. It was that hiss which
helped him to open his eyes. He had no idea
where he was. It was quite dark, except for
a single thin shaft of sunlight which seemed
to have found a crack in the dark roof
above him. The beam was sharp and
golden, and was obviously from the sun
at high noon.

Idly his gaze followed the beam until it
rested in a splash of golden colour on metal-
work, metal-work which was splashed with
yellow burn stains. Then Taffy Morris
remembered. It was like a shuddering blast

of icy wind down his aching spine. The tank! He was in their tank—*Mae West (Come up and see me some time)*. They had named their tank after the famous film star and her famous saying had also been painted on the gun turret.

Taffy tried to get his eyes to focus in the semi-gloom, and though the dull hammering inside his skull was still going on, his brain was clearing. In seconds it all came back. The Knightsbridge cauldron!

The 7th Armoured Division had been battling against the heaviest odds they had ever known. For days, how many days he could not remember now, they had faced the more heavily-armed German Mk. IV tanks. Their own tanks had been badly outranged and outgunned. To add further to their discomfiture, Stuka dive-bombers had screamed out of the sky to harass them relentlessly. Their situation would have been intolerable if it hadn't been for the R.A.F. who were getting in amongst the enemy planes and exacting a heavy toll.

Taffy screwed up his eyes in an effort to remember why they were still here, and why everything was so quiet. He remembered receiving a radio signal. They were to pull out. The whole front line was withdrawing under enormous pressure. He had had to guess at some parts of the message, for Lucky Jordan was firing their 37 mm. gun as fast as he could and German shells had been bursting all around with ear-shattering noise.

"Feeling better, Taffy?"

The voice was like a slap in the face to the Welshman. In the few seconds since his head had begun to clear he had forgotten the singer, and somehow failed to realise that he was not alone in the disabled tank. Lying face down was George, the mechanic/driver/gun-loader. Opposite him was Lucky Jordan—the singer.

"Couldn't feel worse," Taffy croaked, adding: "Unless I was dead. Come to think of it, I might be dead; I don't know. Somebody keeps belting me across the head with a hammer."

"You're not dead," Lucky Jordan assured him, and picking up a water-bottle which had been resting between his legs he held it out, saying: "Here, have a swig—not too much, for that's all we've got."

The water was warm and tasted as if it had been in the bottle for years, but as it went down the Welshman's parched throat it was like life-giving wine. He could feel it spreading out inside him, and within a minute a thick beading of sweat was crawling out on to his forehead. He lifted the bottle again, but Lucky Jordan's big hand took it away.

"Don't forget the diver," he said, slapping the cork on. "There are three of us to drink out of this little lot, and the nearest pub is a long way off—a very long way."

"Pub!" The weak voice seemed to come from nowhere, startling Taffy and Lucky for a moment until the man curled face down beside them somehow uncoiled himself. It was George Dowling, a giant of a man, and when he finally sat up the interior of the tank seemed suddenly even more crowded.

Without a word Lucky Jordan held out the water-bottle. George fumbled for nearly ten seconds before his shaking right hand closed over the cork and pulled it out. He tipped back his head and there was a gurgle-gurgle-gurgle which fascinated Taffy. He wanted to warn George that he was taking all their precious water but he said nothing.

"Cor, luv a duck," sighed George as he tossed the empty bottle over to Jordan and then wiped his mouth with the back of his hand. After a moment he continued breathlessly: "I wish I was a duck. If they threw me in a reservoir I'd drink it dry in ten minutes. Where are we?"

"Well, for the benefit of all concerned," Lucky Jordan said, patting the pockets of his sweat-stained khaki shirt, "we are where we were when the ruddy bomb hit us. Knightsbridge they called the place and I wish I was walking through Knightsbridge back home right now."

"So it was a bomb!" George said, feeling gingerly at the side of his head. "I was just firing at one of Jerry's Mk. IV tanks that had come over the ridge when—phooey."

"Just one big flash," Jordan agreed, "and I was . . ."

"What about Alfie?" Taffy interrupted, pointing to a huddled figure on whose khaki shirt-sleeves were the three stripes of a sergeant.

"I looked at him," Jordan said, shaking

12

a gloomy head. "He's had it, Taff. Bomb splinter, I think. You gets the glory sittin' up in the turret but there's more chance of stoppin' a bit of old iron up there. He's had it. Poor old Alfie."

The other two shrugged. They were sorry, but war was like that. You had a pal one minute, then a bullet, a bomb, or a stray piece of shell casing with your pal's number on it came along and that was it: living one minute, dead the next.

Taffy brought out a crumpled packet, and passed a cigarette to each of his friends. George found matches and they sat smoking and thinking for a little while.

"Is there any grub?" George finally broke the gloomy silence, and was answered by Lucky Jordan with a scornful:

"Grub! Can't you think of anything else?"

"A man has to live," George protested, "and if I don't bother . . ." and there his voice trailed off into silence. He followed the example of his friends who had nipped the glowing ends from their cigarettes. All three could hear something. It sounded like the engines of some powerful vehicle. Perhaps a Mk. IV tank coming round to make sure there was no one left alive in the knocked-out British tanks. It was the usual routine clean-up job.

The General Grant tank in which they were sitting had had a relatively long life as tanks went in the Western Desert. The 7th Armoured Division nicknamed the *Desert Rats* had hammered, and been hammered by, Rommel and the Afrika Korps more than once, but even the best of tanks did not last forever.

The growling of the motor died away. They heard voices. Then came the clank of a nailed boot on the side of the *Mae West*. Lucky Jordan looked round for a weapon, but Taffy with a quick gesture urged him to lie where he was and keep silent. His eyes pleaded: "Lie still. If they think we are dead they might go away. You never know your luck." No one spoke. They knew the routine when a disabled tank was found with its crew alive. There was a curt command to "Come out" and if there was not instant obedience a hand grenade in the right place sent the tank up in flames.

For what seemed an age nothing happened. Then there was a harsh screech of metal on metal. The German on the tank was trying to drag the turret-top open. The bomb blast which had put the General Grant out of action had twisted the turret slightly. The three Britishers could hear the man outside cursing and struggling. Then, with a wail, the tank turret opened and a German looked in.

He drew back after a second or so, waving his hand before his nose.

"All dead, Hans," he called, turning to the big tank transporter vehicle halted some ten yards away. "I'll leave the turret top open, and let some air in. Maybe we should come back later, eh?"

Understanding no more German than *Ja* and *Nein*, the three Britishers remained absolutely still. For a few seconds it seemed as if the miracle might happen. Perhaps the Germans would go away; but the German N.C.O. in charge of the transporter was an old hand in desert warfare.

"We'll have to get them out now," he insisted. "If we leave them the stink will be much worse. The heat inside must be like an oven. Hand them up to me. We'll give them a quick burial. The sand is fairly loose here. It won't take long."

The German on the tank growled his disgust. He put a leg into the turret, took a deep breath of fresh air to protect his lungs as long as possible from the combined smells of old cordite, petrol, oil, and stale air, and slid hurriedly into the tank.

It was George Dowling who hit him. George was the driver/mechanic of the tank, and what he did not know about engines and tanks could have been written on a sixpence and still left room for other things. He was also an expert at close-quarter fighting.

For a man who did not say much and spoke slowly, he was like lightning with his fists. The German never felt a thing. One moment he was bending to get hold of the nearest " body ", and the next he was limp as a wet sack. Taffy and Lucky Jordan stared in goggle-eyed horror.

" Well, for crying out loud," Lucky Jordan whispered. " That's just about the daftest thing anybody could have done. They'll just about murder us by inches for this. If you think . . ."

George lifted a finger to his lips for silence. Someone else was climbing on to the tank. It was the second of the three men working the tank transporter. He was coming to lend a hand in getting the "bodies" out of the tank. The shaft of sunlight shining down into the tank interior was cut off for a second or so as the second German peered in.

"Can you manage the . . . ?" he said, and then gaped. Down there, hard to see at first after being accustomed to the brilliantly harsh light of the desert, was Fritz, and he was lying face down—face down, across the legs of four dead "Tommies."

"Corporal. . . . Fritz has passed out. The air in that tank must be murder. What shall we . . . ?"

"Get in, Joachim," Corporal Hans roared, "but hold your breath." Leaping out of the transporter's seat he rushed across to lend a hand. His first thought had been that the knocked-out British tank must be full of carbon monoxide from the exhaust fumes. This he knew would poison anyone who inhaled it for any length of time.

Corporal Hans scrambling up the tank

heaved himself on to the turret. The head and shoulders of a pale-faced Fritz was just appearing. The corporal, assuming that the unconscious man was being pushed up by Joachim, grabbed hold of him.

Below, George had dealt with the second German as quickly and effectively as he had done with the unfortunate Fritz. Then he had grabbed Fritz and pushed him up to the turret opening. Germans there might be outside the tank, but he wanted some fresh air, and he was ready to fight for the privilege of breathing it again.

Corporal Hans of the German Tank Recovery Unit was unlucky. He had scarcely time to realise that the man leaping out of the tank was not Joachim, when something hit him. Big George had large fists, and he was clutching a grenade in each. They added to his punching powers, and if the German N.C.O. had been struck by a thunderbolt he could not have been knocked out any quicker.

Breathing hard, George looked round for the next man. He had whipped the safety pin from the grenade in his right hand and

Big George had large fists . . .

he dared not let it go until he had found a target; there were no targets.

As he stood looking round, breathing fire and slaughter, he could see wrecked tanks scattered here and there. Some were still giving off a thin film of dirty smoke. Another, a German Mk. IV tank, had its tracks wrapped about it as if some giant had decided to use them as a scarf.

George was still standing there when Taffy and Lucky Jordan joined him. Both were white-faced, each expecting to face Germans armed with pistols or the deadly Schmeisser automatic weapons. Instead they saw only George and the limp Hans lying by the side of the equally limp Fritz.

" Have you killed him?" Taffy asked, a nervous stutter in his voice.

" Never mind that." Lucky Jordan sized up the situation in a flash. He saw the grenade pin still clutched in George's teeth and his eyes goggled. He took the pin, carefully inserted it back in the grenade and heaved a sigh of relief. George was a good pal to have in a scrap, but he was apt to be careless with grenades.

" Now what do we do?" George asked,

stuffing one grenade into each pocket of his dusty trousers.

"Get these two tied up—and gagged," Lucky said, looking at Taffy. Then to George "Get the other bloke out of the tank. We don't want him coming round and lobbing old iron at us. There are some of our grenades in there, you know."

George nodded and scrambled back into the tank. Lucky looked around and frowned when he saw a slight movement on the top of the ridge less than quarter of a mile away. He cupped his hands about his eyes to shut out the dazzling glare of the sun on the yellow sand. After staring for a few moments his frown deepened. Unless he was mistaken, another German Tank Recovery Unit was over there, getting ready to salvage one of their battered Mk. IV tanks.

George reappeared in the turret pushing the limp Joachim ahead of him. He hauled the man down and laid him alongside Fritz and Hans. Meanwhile Taffy had been looking over the big tank transporter, and he came round now with a jerrycan. His eyes were gleaming.

"Water," he said, and because he was the

most unselfish of men, he handed the big can to George.

"Strike a light!" George's eyes glistened. He opened the jerrycan, poured a couple of pints of the tepid water over his head and shoulders, then drank.

"Eh, you're not a flipping sink," Taffy protested as George gulped and gulped.

"Is that the only water there is?" Lucky asked. "There'll be more, surely."

He was right, and Taffy reappeared staggering under the weight of two more full jerrycans. It was the turn of the Welshman and Lucky Jordan to sluice their heads in water before gulping down more than a pint of water each.

By this time Fritz was beginning to mumble and make weak movements with his hands. Taffy darted away and came back with a length of rope. This was cut into shorter pieces and with them the three Germans were securely tied up.

"Better gag them, too," Lucky suggested.

"Gag them," Taffy said, startled. "You have been watching too many gangster films, Lucky. What do we want to gag them for? Who's going to hear them anyway?"

"Over there," Lucky said grimly, and with a jerk of his thumb indicated the second German Tank Recovery Unit. "They might come this way, and you know the old saying: 'Silence is golden.'"

Taffy and George squinted across the dazzling dusty surface of the desert and nodded. Then George turned and looked at their three prisoners. The effects of his terrific punches were wearing off.

"What are we going to do with this little lot?" he asked, and rubbed at his bristly chin, and as the sound reminded him he was unshaven, he said: "Blimey, I need a shave. I feel like an old shoe-brush."

"We could shoot 'em," Lucky said, watching the faces of the three Germans intently. A moment later he was standing over the N.C.O. "So you understand English, eh? And don't lie. . . . I saw you sort of flinch when I said we could shoot you. You do speak English, don't you?"

"*Ja—ja!*" the German agreed, "a little. Just a little."

"That's all we need," Lucky said. "Now I'm going to ask you some questions. . . ." He was interrupted then and there by Taffy.

"Lucky . . . those Jerries are coming this way I think," and he jerked a thumb towards the distant ridge.

All three Britishers turned and stared in the direction of the ridge. There seemed no doubt that Taffy was right. The Recovery crew had got their Mk. IV tank loaded, and there was a rising cloud of dust behind the big, lumbering vehicle, indicating it was on the move. They watched for a minute, hoping the tank transporter might turn round and head west, for that was the direction Rommel and his Afrika Korps had come from. Instead, to their dismay, the dust began to move in their direction.

"Think our gun will be all right?" Taffy asked.

"Don't be nuts!" Lucky said tartly, and stood for a few moments scratching at his dust-filled hair. Then he shrugged. "George nip in and see if our engines are still running. Taffy, help me get this bloke out of sight," and he indicated the terrified Joachim.

They hauled him on to the tank transporter, laid him under the hawser reel and Lucky then dropped a length of oily sacking over him. The sacking was used to keep the desert dust out of the winch mechanism.

"And this bloke?" Taffy asked, indicating Hans, the N.C.O.

"Take his gag out," Lucky ordered, and from his own pocket he took a grenade. He stood idly tossing it from hand to hand, watched by the ashen-faced Hans. "Now take the rope off his wrists."

"Eh?"

"I said take the rope off his wrists," Lucky repeated. "Oh, don't bother, go and get the other bloke's peaked cap. You might as well look as much like a Jerry as you can. I'll see to this other fellow," pointing at Fritz.

He helped the dazed German to his feet, herded him on to the transporter and ordered him to lie down beside the now hatless Joachim. He threw the sacking back over both of them. When he got round to the cab of the transporter, Hans, the N.C.O., had been freed by Taffy and was standing sullenly facing them.

"Now, this laddie is going to help us get the tank on to the transporter," Lucky said.

"You mess about as if you were helping, Taffy. Keep as much out of sight as you can. We'll have that other crew here in a few minutes. Oh . . . climb up and tell George what we are doing. Better tell him to swing the gun round. If things get out of hand . . . he can give 'em a bellyfull. He'll like that."

Then he turned to the anxious Hans. He held out the grenade, saying :

"If your blokes come here, you'd better talk nice and smooth. If things go wrong I'm going to slip this down the back of your shirt—after I've pulled the pin out. Get me?" And to show what he meant, he spun Hans round and in one swift movement had got his hand down the neck of the sweat-stained shirt, letting the terrified German feel the hardness of the grenade he held.

"*Ja—ja*, I understand!" Hans muttered, and went on hurriedly. "I will make no mistake. You will see. I will make no mistake at all."

Taffy, who had been talking down the turret top to George, jumped down to announce :

"He's got the turret working, and he's loaded up."

"Right, you shove round to the back, and we'll start getting our tank on. If anybody gets near enough to speak, don't say anything. I'll do the talking."

"You'll do the . . ." Taffy began, his eyes narrowing. "I didn't know you spoke German. I . . ."

"I don't," Lucky said, grinning, and nudging the nervous Hans in the ribs. "We've got a good friend here who's only too anxious to help. That's right, isn't it?" he demanded, his voice suddenly harsh and threatening.

"*Ja— ja*, I will help," Hans hastened to assure him.

The German climbed into the cab, started the engine, and began to swing the cumbersome transporter round so that the ramp would be in position for hauling the British tank aboard. Lucky watched, tossing the grenade from hand to hand, but never taking his eyes off the German N.C.O.

"I must get down, now," the sweating Hans said, dragging on his brake and switching the engine over to the winch mechanism.

With the second German transporter lumbering nearer all the time, the two Britishers and Hans dragged the heavy wire cables across to the disabled tank, and hooked them on. Then Hans strode up the ramp with Lucky at his heels. By now the other vehicle, with its battered Mk. IV tank aboard, had swung to a dusty halt some fifty yards away, while the man in the cab leaned out and yelled something.

" Start the winch up," Lucky ordered.

" He wants to speak to me," Hans stuttered, his eyes goggling in terror.

" Do you want to die?" Lucky asked, hooking his thumb into the grenade safety pin ring. " You answer him. Make it short and sweet, then start the winch. If they come across here, matey, you've had it. Know what that means?"

" *Ja!* " Hans understood the phrase well enough. Sweat rolled down his dust-covered face. The German realised he was as near death now as he ever would be. One false move and this Britisher would blast them both into Eternity.

Hans yelled something to the second Recovery Unit crew, then hurried to the winch gear mechanism and put the machinery in gear. There were convulsive wriggles from beneath the sacking at his feet as Fritz and Joachim tried to move away. They were in no danger, for the tank could not be hauled up that far; but, unable to see because of the sacking, they were half-crazed with terror.

Lucky Jordan stopped their wriggling. He leaned forward and poked each in turn in the ribs with a stiff forefinger. It must have felt to the frightened Germans like the muzzle of a pistol, for their wriggling ceased immediately.

At that moment one of the men from the other transporter got out of his cab and started walking towards them. Taffy, who had been dodging about on the other side of the tank trying to look as industrious as possible, spotted him and rushed to Lucky with the news.

" What do we do now?" he yelled at the top of his voice. With the grinding of the winch mechanism, the screech and groan of tank's tracks sliding on to the ramp leading to the transporter's platform, ordinary speech was impossible.

Lucky waved a hand to indicate that Taffy should be silent. The German was now less than ten yards away, and slowing down as he watched the disabled British tank slide steadily into place. A few moments later the roar of the engine died down as the winch was slipped out of gear.

The approaching German called up something to the trembling Hans, and before Lucky realised what was happening he was alone. Hans had jumped off the transporter.

2. Rommel's uninvited guests

IN THE NEXT FEW SECONDS the fate of nine men hung in the balance. In the British tank George had surreptitiously swung the muzzle of his gun round until it covered the other German tank transporter. Lucky Jordan, caught off balance for only a split second, brought his hand round like a whip-lash, but the grenade which he had been holding in case of an emergency never left his grasp.

The German N.C.O. was no fool. He was frightened, but he knew enough about hand grenades to realise that when he jumped he would have four, perhaps five seconds before Lucky's grenade exploded. In that time Hans reckoned he could run along the side of the transporter and perhaps throw himself under its bonnet.

It was a good idea, but it was not the German's lucky day. As he jumped, a loose steel toe-protector on his right boot caught in his left legging. It slashed the thin webbing as if it had been a knife. The momentary jerk threw Hans off balance. He stumbled forward. The German waiting to speak to him stretched out his hands to catch and steady the falling Hans.

Hans was so afraid that the mad Britisher would then blow them all to kingdom come that he changed his mind about running for safety. He balanced himself with one hand on the shoulder of the other N.C.O. and lifting his right boot looked glumly at the protruding boot protector. He twisted it to and fro a few times until the wafer-thin metal broke. He tossed it on to the sand and said shakily :

" Must get my boots repaired, or I'll be hurting myself."

He accepted a cigarette and light, throwing a quick glance over his shoulder as he did so. Lucky Jordan was still there, lounging against the end of the tank, his left hand busy mopping sweat from his dust-yellowed face. His right hand was on his hip and held in such a way that the lethal grenade was concealed.

The two Germans talked for a minute or so, Hans saying little more than a nervous " Yes " or " No ". The other N.C.O. had come across to pass on the information that the Tank Repair Unit had moved up. The British were withdrawing all along the line, and Rommel wanted his tanks under repair as far east as possible, to be ready for the next big action.

When they parted, Hans stood for a few moments sucking at his cigarette, and finally Lucky with a jerk of his head ordered the German to return to the transporter cab. As Hans turned, Lucky dropped lightly off the transporter and followed him.

When he was seated in the cab by the German's side he said jocularly:

"I thought for a moment you were going to make a dash for it. Were you?"

"No, no, no." Hans protested. "I jumped down so that Hermann—the N.C.O. from the other tank transporter would not come any closer."

"Very friendly of you, I'm sure," Lucky said, grinning. "And what do we do now?"

"We go to Acruma. The Tank Repair Unit has moved up. All tank repairs will be done in Acruma until we are ready to move on to Alexandria, then Cairo and Suez."

In his right hand was the grenade ...

"Good-ho," Lucky said approvingly. "It's very nice in Alex. You'll like it."

Hans shot him a quick glance. The trouble with these Britishers was that you never could understand them. This man should be worried, but he was smiling, as if the idea of Rommel and the Afrika Korps pushing the British out beyond the Suez Canal was the nicest thing he had heard for a long time.

Dropping his hand to the gear-lever the German disengaged the winch engine and was about to put the tank transporter itself in forward gear when Lucky laid a hand on his.

"We'll wait, I think," he said gently. "We'll follow them. Its rude to push yourself to the front, you know. Always let the other fellow go first."

Hans shook his head, and fresh beads of perspiration broke out on his forehead.

"I am ordered to lead the way," he said anxiously. "I have been over the ground before. I know the way. See . . . this badge," and he tapped a small cloth badge on his right arm. "I am ordered to lead."

It was a blow for Lucky. He had thought

that if the other tank transporter got moving, raising the inevitable cloud of rolling yellow dust, he and his two comrades might be able to slip away. It would mean stopping the transporter and putting this big blond German out of action, but that would not have been difficult.

He gave the German a long, hard stare which brought new fear to the man's eyes. Hans blew out a sigh of relief when Lucky finally said :

" Okay, get moving."

There was a crunch from the gear-box, then they started the long haul to Acruma. It was twenty-five miles away, and the tank transporters could not do more than about five miles an hour over the desert. In some places the winds had blown the sand clear away, leaving a rock-hard clay, in others the sand was deep, and soft as a feather cushion. The going would be slow and difficult for the heavily-laden transporters.

When they had been going for about five minutes Lucky moved across to the opposite side of the cab and looked back. Through the clouds of yellow dust he could vaguely see the second transporter away to one side.

Taking a chance, Lucky yelled:

" Taffy . . . TAFFY. Come here."

Taffy on the transporter platform, wormed his way along and finally got to the outside of the cab.

" What's the drill now, Lucky?" he demanded. " We can't make a run for it. That other Jerry transporter isn't more than a hundred yards behind. Are you going to look for a *wadi*, where we could try and run for it?"

" Be your age, Taff," Lucky countered. " They've got a short-wave radio in the cab here. They'll have one in the other transporter. If we made a dash for it they'd have one of their spotter aircraft out looking for us before you could say ' Jack Robinson '. Hang on. Tell George to see if our engines are in running order. If we got half a chance I wouldn't mind trying to get back under our own steam."

" What! You must be nuts," Taffy said. Then he left the cab, made his way back to the transporter platform and climbed into the tank where he found George amusing himself by keeping his gun lined up on the transporter coming up behind them.

"Is he going to have a go at them?" George asked, his eyes lighting up. "I could knock the guts out of that thing behind us with two shots."

"He's crazy," Taffy growled. "Know what he said. 'Tell George to see if his engines are in running order. If we got half a chance I wouldn't mind trying to get back under our own steam.' Think of it, George . . . trying to run this wreck back to the British lines."

"Yeah!" George's big blue eyes narrowed almost to slits as he thought of it. To him it seemed a good idea. He looked up at Taffy sitting on the rim of the hatch and said: "Lucky has some good ideas, Taff. Cor, strike a light! Just imagine us driving through the Jerry lines and reporting back to our own mob. They *would* call us the Desert Rats, wouldn't they? It's worth trying." And he eased himself out of the gunner's seat and turned to the engines.

"You're as daft as him," Taffy snarled. "Walk home; Yes! I'd have a go at that any time. But take this ruddy tank back? You couldn't do it in a month of blue Sundays. Have some sense, George."

George looked round and up for a moment, and there was a slow smile on his face as he said:

"You know, Taff, even third class riding is better than first class walking. I'm not one of those blokes who go wearing their boots away, walking. If I can ride back . . . that's what I'm going to do. You should . . ." and he stopped there for there was no one to listen to him. The disgusted Taffy had slid his legs out of the turret top and gone down to the transporter platform, to sit by the side of the two prisoners. He had taken pity on them and dragged the oily hessian from their faces so that they could breathe better.

Taffy's spirits sank lower and lower as they neared Acruma. Since they were following closely the route taken by the advancing Panzer divisions, he saw ample evidence of the struggle which had taken place before the British finally pulled out. Tanks and armoured cars lay burning where they had been hit and German working parties were everywhere, collecting the wounded and burying the dead. Rommel had driven the

British back, but he had paid a heavy price for his success.

When Hans saw these unmistakable signs of a victory he became quite cheerful and confident. It was only when he shot a sideways glance at Lucky Jordan that his face grew thoughtful again.

Through the five hour journey Lucky sat with the grenade in his right hand, the safety pin in his left. It was a grim warning of what would happen should Hans try any tricks. The Britisher need only open his right hand. If he did that the spring-loaded release lever would flick away, and within seconds the grenade would explode.

Three times they passed within a dozen yards of German soldiers who were collecting arms and ammunition for loading on to lorries. One word from Hans would have meant certain capture and imprisonment for the three Britishers. But Hans would have died too, and so he merely waved to men who called across to them. Then, as the sun dropped out of sight behind them and the twilight settled over the desert, they came to Acruma.

"What do you do now?" Hans asked, when they crawled up behind a queue of vehicles waiting to enter a wired-off enclosure. There a small army of mechanics and technicians were working furiously to repair damaged tanks, armoured cars and lorries.

"We'll go in," Lucky said. "I expect they'll direct you to some place, won't they?"

"*Ja!* Those tanks which are easily repaired are put in one section of the enclosure and the more badly damaged ones are put in another, to be looked at when there is more time." Hans was beginning to worry again. If this lean-jawed Britisher had shown the slightest sign of apprehension, Hans would have felt better. But the man sat there as calm, and apparently unconcerned, as if he was waiting to enter a British enclosure.

The queue moved nearer the enclosure and a German was passing along from transporter to transporter, handing out a paper to each driver. One was thrust in to Hans, and for a moment Lucky thought the German with the papers stared suspiciously into the cab. It was only Lucky's imagination for the man moved on at once.

"This I must fill in," Hans said, indicating the form, and before Lucky could ask any questions, went on: "It is to say what kind of vehicle we bring in, and if it is badly damaged."

"Okay," Lucky was thinking hard. "Fill in that it is badly damaged. Here, let me have a look at it." He took the paper and pretended to study it, while Hans watched him closely, wondering if this Britisher could read German. If he could not, then there was a chance that he could get a message out, for the form would be collected in the next few minutes.

"Yeah, I see," Lucky said, turning the form over, and pretending to study the instructions on the back. Suddenly he thrust the form back to Hans, saying: "Fill it in . . . and say this tank is badly damaged, see? Very badly damaged. And . . . ouch!" He made a sudden movement as if he had almost let the grenade slip from his fingers.

The German's face turned the colour of putty, and the shock unnerved him so much that he dropped the form, and had to fumble hurriedly for it at his feet.

"If I got a shock I *might* drop it," Lucky said, grinning. "So don't make any mistakes. If you put one wrong word on that form . . . this little beauty goes right inside your shirt."

Five minutes later the form, hurriedly filled in, was collected. There was another ten minute wait, then they were directed to a part of the enclosure where badly hit Mk. IV tanks and a few British ones were parked side by side. They would be given a quick inspection next day to decide whether they were worth attempting to repair. Men were at work guiding the transporters to the various "parks", and one of them, after checking the vehicle Hans was driving, guided them with a masked torch to an empty spot.

When they were in position to begin offloading, he came round to have a word with the driver. He pulled open the door and looked in, and after asking if they had heard the latest battle news, told Hans how far back the British had been driven.

When he had finished he said :

"There is a letter post going in a few minutes. Have you any letters?"

Hans had a card. He handed it over and the man then asked Lucky if he had any mail. Having no idea at all what the man was saying, Lucky merely grunted.

"I asked if you had any mail," the German repeated and lifted his torch to shine the beam on Lucky's face. It was then that a completely unexpected thing gave the game away. Lucky Jordan's shirt was unbuttoned, exposing his chest; the Britisher had never been fond of sun-bathing, so his chest showed white, and there was a tattoo design on it.

The torch beam lit up Lucky's chest for a moment, then moved up to make the taut-faced Britisher screw up his eyes. A second later, however, the beam was lowered again so that it shone on the V-shaped expanse of exposed chest. There, clear and sharp in the light were the two intertwined hearts, and round them, tattooed in red, were the words "I love Joan."

Like many of the Germans who had hoped to take part in the invasion of Britain, this man had taken a course in English, and had been an apt pupil. He spoke the language well, and could also read English. His brow furrowed into a frown as he read the tattooed phrase " I love Joan."

" I love Joan," he said, puzzled. " But those words are English. Why do you have . . . ?" And then suddenly suspicious, he moved his torch so that the light shone where every German, whether he was infantryman, airman, or even a humble cook, carried the insignia of his unit. Lucky had earlier taken the precaution of ripping off his own regimental markers.

Even more suspicious than before, the German turned to Hans with an angry :

" Who is this man? How long has he been with you? Is he dumb?"

Poor Hans gulped noisily. Lucky Jordan had pressed the hand gripping the grenade hard against the unhappy German's back. It was a silent warning which Hans dared not ignore.

" I . . . I . . ." Hans could not think. He did not know what to say, and his obvious terror confirmed the suspicions of the man hanging on to the cab door that there was something wrong. He was drawing back a pace, meaning to bring someone in authority, when Lucky made a grab for him.

The Britisher had to lean across Hans, and it was the chance the German N.C.O. had been praying for. He made a quick grab for the Britisher's fist, meaning to snatch the live grenade from him. His action spoiled Lucky's grab, and he was inches short of getting a grip on the German's tunic collar.

With a yelp of anger mingled with fear the man turned and began to run. Now he was certain there was something wrong. Stories had been circulating for some time of bands of British terrorists who were working behind the German lines. Staging posts on the roads had been shot up, airfields raided, lorries held up and then blown up, This German was convinced that he had innocently guided a gang of these crazy British desperadoes right into the middle of their tank park.

"*Achtung!*" he screamed, "*Ach* . . ." and then he went down with a crash which shook the air from his lungs. Out of the darkness alongside the big transporter a shadowy figure had come. It was Taffy

Morris. If he had made such a dive on a Welsh rugby football ground he would have had half the male population of Wales bursting their lungs singing " Land of our fathers ". Alas for Taffy, there was no one to see that super tackle, but it did everything Taffy wanted. It brought the terrified German down with a crunch which left him paralysed for the next few seconds. Then Taffy pounced on him as a starving cat pounces on a mouse. Taffy was small, and lean, but he was a hard hitter.

While the Welshman was making sure the German did not get up for some time, a short and bitter struggle was going on in the transporter's cab. When Hans had made his grab the live grenade dropped from Lucky's hand.

" You crazy nit," Lucky snarled, and jabbing his left elbow in the German's throat reached down with his right hand in a desperate attempt to retrieve the grenade before it was too late.

It was too late to make the grenade safe again. The spring loaded lever had been flicked away, the firing pin had gone down, and within seconds the tightly packed explosives inside would rip the grenade apart.

Groping fingers found the grenade, and Lucky Jordan flipped it through the open door of the cab. It was a marvellous effort, and fear gave Lucky additional strength. The moment the grenade was gone he hurled himself backwards out of the cab, his hands going to his head in an automatic effort to shield his close-cropped head from flying fragments. Hans fell on top of him, and he too had his shoulders hunched, waiting for the crack and the whistling hail of hot metal. Britisher and German knew the lethal power of a grenade at close-quarters.

There was a "clang" as the grenade struck the top of the next vehicle, a battered Mk. IV tank. The grenade started to bounce off, and exploded as it did so. There was a sudden, brilliant flash which lit up the Tank Recovery Park. There was the sharp whip-like crack of the explosion, then a devil's tattoo as fragments of metal rattled against tanks and armoured cars before screaming off into the night in frightening ricochets.

It was all over within seconds: the flash, the bang, the clangs, the screeches, the

There was a sudden brilliant flash ...

silence. Until then there had been a continual murmur of sound over the big enclosure.

The silence which followed the bursting of the grenade was almost overpowering. Even Hans, half-winded on the ground by the side of Lucky, did not move. For almost a minute it seemed as if everything and everyone had died. The Royal Air Force had a nasty habit of suddenly swooping out of the sky and beating up Rommel's repair units and his airfields, so this sudden, unexpected explosion made everyone think a British plane was overhead.

A whistle shrilled. It was the German air-raid warning signal, and every man who had not already switched off his torch, did so immediately. Men dived for the cover of tanks and armoured cars, and waited for the next bomb to come screaming down.

Lucky Jordan got over the shock before Hans. He rolled to his knees, and for the second time in less than twelve hours, the unlucky German felt the power of a British fist. Hans struggled, but a punch in the solar plexus ended the struggle. Lucky turned the man face down, whipped his arms round his back and secured them with the German's own belt.

"Psst!" It was Taffy. "That you, Lucky?"

"Yes," Lucky was panting a little. "Get hold of George. We've got to beat it. Somebody's goin' to find out soon that there are no planes overhead. Who's that you have there?"

"He was running away from the truck," Taffy explained. "I thought it was the driver. What shall I do with him?"

"You could sit holding his hands," Lucky said sarcastically. "Tie him up, you clot, and gag him. Then chuck him under a lorry where he won't be seen."

He followed his own advice with Hans, tearing the man's shirt into strips to provide a gag and material for ankle lashings. By the time he had finished there were signs that the Germans were getting over their surprise following the explosion. In the breathless silence which lay over the scene, scores of men looked upwards and strained to catch even à hint of sound from an enemy aircraft. There was nothing.

Almost ten minutes went by before the

"all clear" whistle sounded, for there was scarcely a man in the Tank Recovery and Repair Unit who had not experienced the R.A.F.'s *silent approach* method. Light bombers operating far behind the German lines would switch off their engines, then glide silently down, drop their bombs, and be gone before anyone could fire a gun. With their diving speed to help them they could be miles away before they needed to switch on power again. Often they repeated the manœuvre, and the Germans paid a high price for switching on their lights too soon.

By the time the "all clear" whistle was blown Lucky had found Taffy, and the two men went to the tank transporter.

He climbed on to the General Grant, poked his head into the turret and whispered:

"George, are you there?"

"Yeah!"

"Well, come on out, you mop-headed clot. We've gotta get out of here quick. Didn't you hear the explosion? Half the German army will be here in a minute, looking for us. If we can ..."

"Lucky," George did not usually allow things to worry him, but there was a note of anxiety in his voice now. "What are we going to do about Alfie?"

"Alfie! Oh, for pete's sake, George. What do you want to do: fire six rounds over him and sound 'The Last Post'? If we . . ."

"He isn't dead," George butted in.

"What!" It was not often Lucky Jordan was robbed of speech, but he was now. When he first came round after the bomb explosion which had put them all out of action, he had looked at Alfie. He had seen the wound, and had been satisfied that their tank commander had "bought it". In an awed whisper Jordan finally said: "But he was deader than last week's mutton. I'm sure he was."

"You were wrong, Lucky." The words floated up from the darkness of the tank. The voice was weak, but there was no doubt who the speaker was.

"Strike a light," Lucky murmured, and climbed into the tank, with Taffy almost treading on the top of his head. Taffy swung the turret top in place as quietly as

56

he could, then switched on the torch he had taken from the German who had almost given the alarm.

There was a grin on George's face as he knelt by the side of the wounded Alfie.

"I was checking the damage, and I thought I heard a sound. It was Alfie, so I gave him a drink."

Lucky Jordan dropped to one knee and stared at the wounded man. War in the desert had made Jordan tough. He was as hard-bitten as only a real Desert Rat could be, but there was a lump in his throat now as he stared at their tank commander. Though none of them would have admitted it, they would have followed Alfie Dimmer anywhere. Lucky cleared his throat. "It's my fault," he finally managed to say. "I was so sure you were a goner. I suppose I didn't take a real look."

"We all make mistakes, Lucky," Alfie said weakly. "Anyway, where are we and what's going on? I thought I heard something explode a minute or so ago."

"Aye, what happened?" George added his plea for information.

Taffy got in first, telling the story of the

day in a burst of Welsh eloquence which somehow made the whole thing sound unreal.

"And we're slap in the middle of a Jerry repair compound now," Lucky Jordan managed to get in a word when Taffy had to pause for breath. "I was just going to drag old George here out, so we could get mobile before it was too late. I reckon that whistle was their 'all clear', and you can bet your last boot-lace they'll start looking round to see what caused the rumpus."

Sergeant Alfie Dimmer nodded.

"That's the best thing," he agreed weakly. "You'll report me wounded and a prisoner-of-war when you get back, won't you? I wouldn't like the folks at home to think I was a dead duck."

"Er . . . but we're not going now," Lucky said hesitantly, adding at once. "I mean . . . we wouldn't leave you here, Sarge. If . . ."

"You can't take me with you, that's a fact," Alfie pointed out quietly. "I can't walk, and I know you couldn't carry me. No, its been nice knowing you, and I wish you the best of luck. I hope you make it. Well, I know you will," and he held out a shaking right hand to Jordan.

"Look, Sarge, we're not leav . . ." Lucky began, only to be interrupted. Sergeant Alfie Dimmer had no wish to be taken prisoner, but he knew what the odds were. He shook his head, saying:

"It's nice of you, Lucky, but you can't do it. Get out while you can, and the best of luck. You'll need it."

He shook hands with Lucky, then with Taffy, then with George. Big George looked bewildered. He scratched at his dust-filled hair before saying:

"Look, Sarge, we can't do without you. I won't do it. If we . . ."

"You *will* do it, George," was the quiet retort. "Better for three fit men to get back to our lines, than three fit men and one wounded man to be turned into mincemeat by the first Jerry machine-gunner who has a go at us. You couldn't hope to get me out of here anyway. I can't walk. I appreciate the thought, George. Mebbe we'll meet in Civvy street when it's all over. Leave me some water." He managed a grin, gave them a shaky wave of the hand, then closed his eyes. He opened them after a few seconds when he realised that there had been no movement from the three tank men. Summoning up all the strength left in him, he snapped:

"Jordan, I'm ordering you to get out. I'm putting you in command. Get back to our lines. That's an order."

"Okay, Sarge!" Bleak-eyed, Lucky Jordan motioned Taffy to switch off his torch, then with a slight squeak of metal on metal he pushed up the turret top and climbed out. Taffy followed him. George gave a great sigh, dropped to one knee and laying a hand gently on Sergeant Alfred Dimmer's shoulder said:

"I'm sorry . . . Sarge. I . . ."

"Don't waste time, George," Sergeant Dimmer urged, and patted George's big hand. "I'll come through all right, you'll see. I don't die easily."

"Hope not," George whispered, and climbed out of the tank. A few moments later the turret top creaked down into place again, and the wounded tank commander was alone.

3. Jordan pushes his luck

STANDING BY THE SIDE of the big transporter
the three Britishers were silent for several
minutes. They had expected a massive
search to be taking place, and were amazed
to discover that the activities which the
grenade explosion had stopped so abruptly,
were now going on as if nothing had happened.

What they had overlooked was the fact
that no one suspected the presence of British
troops in the enclosure, and since many of
the tanks contained ammunition, it was
taken for granted that a vehicle or a tank
had come in with a booby mine attached.
It had gone off and since there had been no
cries for help after the explosion, and
apparently no damage, all that had happened
had been a quick inspection in the area
where the explosion had taken place. The
same thing could have happened behind
the British lines under the cloak of darkness.
Every man was concerned with repairing
tanks and armoured cars. Rommel had filled

them all with thoughts of a quick victory. Alexandria, Suez, Cairo, they were all just ahead and the *Desert Fox* (Rommel) needed his armour for the next, and final phase of the campaign.

"We could walk out of here as easy as kissing your hand." Lucky broke the silence which had lain over the three. "If I . . . now, what the flipping heck is that?" The sound which had startled him was a metallic hammering, like someone banging on an enamelled plate.

For a few moments the hammering went on, then stopped as suddenly as it had begun. In response to this signal, work on tanks and other armoured vehicles ceased. The clank of hammers and the clink of spanners died away. By the flashes of a number of masked torches it became obvious that work was finishing. It was left to George to guess the real significance of the signal.

"Grub up," he said. "That was the cookhouse call. Cor, and am I hungry. Wonder what they're having?" and he wiped his mouth with the back of his hairy hand.

When neither Lucky nor Taffy made any comment, George went on speculatively: "Y'know, Lucky, I'll bet we could draw rations like the rest of 'em."

"Don't be daft!" Lucky said, only to have Taffy say:

"I dunno, though, Lucky. If we wear the Afrika Korps peaked caps, how are they to know who we are? You won't have to say anything . . . leastways, not if they dish out grub like our lot do in camp. You just take your mess-tin up, and . . ."

"And nobody notices that it's a British style mess-tin!" Lucky jeered. "Come off it, Taff. Think again."

Taffy shrugged and had no answer to that; but George had. George was hungry, and the thought of a mess-tin piled high with hot food always helped him to think. He had an idea almost immediately, and turning to Lucky said eagerly:

"What about the mess-tins belonging to these blokes from the transporter. They'll have their kit with them, mess-tin and *irons* (knife, fork and spoon). We could borrow those." Then as Lucky did not reply,

George went on almost pathetically: "We've got to eat. We can't walk out of here with empty bellies. I can't anyway."

"Who said we were walking out of here, anyway?" Lucky asked dourly.

"Well, we're not staying here," Taffy said hotly, and added: "At least, I'm not. Me a prisoner-of-war! Not while I've got my boots on."

"We're not *walking* out!" Lucky insisted. "If we walk out it'll mean leaving Alfie. Holy smoke, you don't mean you really thought of leaving him here. Or did you?"

"He said we had to do it," George pointed out. "He's the sarge, isn't he?"

Lucky turned to the little Welshman.

"See if you can find the Jerry mess-tins and eating irons. You stay here, George, and keep your eyes skinned. I'll be back in a minute."

It was more than a minute before he returned, and by that time Taffy had discovered the mess-tins and irons of the tank transporter crew. When Lucky came back he had two pairs of the high-laced boots which the transporter crew had worn. He

"There's nothing like a bit o' dressing up . . ."

tossed one pair down in front of Taffy and dropped the other pair at his own feet.

"There's nothing like a bit o' dressing up," he said grimly. "Wear a Jerry cap and Jerry boots, and nobody's going to look at you twice."

"And what about me?" George asked.

"If you didn't have feet as big as coal barges I might have got a pair for you," and now Lucky was grinning. "Anyway, not to worry. Me and Taff will get extra large helpings, and we'll divide with you and Alfie. I wouldn't like to leave this place unguarded, and you'll do as a sentry. Keep under cover, though, unless somebody comes around and looks like poking in where they shouldn't. Okay?"

"Hm!" George did not sound very happy. As Taffy and Lucky finished lacing up their borrowed boots he said: "Mind you get as much as you can. I'm that hungry I could eat a mule."

"And its harness?" Lucky asked, grinning. "Don't forget the harness. Come on, Taff."

They marched off down the untidy ranks of damaged armour, and across to where men were queueing for the evening meal. As they went, Lucky banged his mess-tin with his fork like a man without a care in the world.

While they were gone George discovered the two Germans who had been lying on the transporter, beneath the big winch. He brought a jerrycan, and untying one man at a time, allowed them to drink their fill. It was an act of mercy which saved the men. Had they been left until the next day they might well have died from heat-stroke.

To pass the time away he checked the water in the tank's cooling system and looked at the tracks. They seemed undamaged, though he would not know for sure until they tried to move it. George was a slow thinker most of the time, but he had an idea what Lucky meant when he said they were not walking home, and not leaving Alfie behind.

" I'm glad we're not leaving him," he murmured to himself. " I'd have felt bad about that. He's a good bloke."

After what seemed an age two shadowy figures appeared near the big transporter. George had already moved to one side, ready to leap in if the two men were Germans. As they came nearer he saw that it was Lucky and Taffy. The smell of cooked food brought him rushing out towards them.

"Like taking pennies off a blind man's plate," Lucky boasted. "Bet you could stay here for a week and they'd never notice you. I always thought the Jerries were sort of reserved, but they're like a flock o' magpies, aren't they Taff?"

"Talking all the time," the little Welshman agreed. "Made me wish I could speak the lingo. Bet they're talking about pushing our lads back."

George opened up the tank and climbed in. There was no sound from Sergeant Dimmer, but when the first mess-tin of food was handed down, bringing with it a mouth-watering smell, he guessed who it was.

"You crazy lunatics," he said. "Why did you come back?"

"Them who don't ask questions get no lies," George assured him, chuckling. "You didn't think we were going to leave you, Sarge, not seriously, eh?"

With the turret top down and the German torch giving them sufficient light to

share out the food, they had their first meal
of the day. They enjoyed it down to the
last drop of gravy. It was washed down
with water, and then they had a smoke.
Sergeant Dimmer was feeling much better,
though he was still very weak. Taffy had
bandaged up the ugly wound in his side but
he would need hospital treatment before he
commanded a tank again.

When he was finishing his cigarette Sergeant Dimmer tried to persuade his three
men to abandon the idea of taking the tank
away.

"You'll never do it," he insisted. "And
why waste your lives? You can help me out
of the tank, and I'll be on my way back to
a German Field Dressing station soon after
daylight."

"Before daylight, Alfie," Lucky told him,
"you'll be on your way back to a British
hospital. You'll like it much better in Cairo
—and maybe we'll be able to come and see
you. Think o' that."

Sergeant Dimmer changed his tactics.

"Look, Jordan, I'm ordering you to get
me out of this tank, then clear off. I don't
care what you do after you've left me—

though I hope you'll try and get back to our lines. Anyway, that's the drill, and you'll do it."

Lucky changed his tactics, too.

"Look, Alfie," he said. "It isn't so long ago you said to me, "I'm putting you in command. Okay, I'm in command. Acting unpaid Sergeant Jordan; but I'm in command. You handed over to me, and both George and Taff will do as *I* say, not what *you* say. George check how much petrol we have. Taff . . . you'll come with me. We'll need all the petrol we can get—and other things. We've got to see if there are any other British tanks here."

"I'll have you in the guardroom for this, Jordan," Dimmer threatened. "You know what this is—refusing to obey the order of a superior officer. You can be court-martialled for it."

"And who in pete's name is going to shoot me if I get this tank back to the British lines?" Jordan demanded truculently. Then with a laugh: "Come off it, Sarge. We're going to have a bash at getting home . . . and you are coming with us. Give him another cig, George. We'll be seeing you."

For the next four hours the work of re-fuelling the General Grant tank *Mae West* went on unobserved. Round the clock, work was going on in the park where the less seriously damaged armour was. But in this part, where every tank, armoured car and lorry was thought to be seriously damaged, no one moved—except Lucky Jordan and Taffy.

With a long piece of rubber hose they siphoned off jerrycan after jerrycan of petrol from tanks and lorries. They carted ammunition from three badly damaged British tanks—they even carried across spare food and water. When Lucky Jordan ran out of ideas, Taffy came up with ideas of his own as to what they could use.

Finally they were ready. George was confident that neither engine was damaged. He had looked again at the tank's tracks, and could find nothing wrong. The bomb which had put the crew of *Mae West* temporarily out of action seemed to have lifted the tank bodily, then dropped it heavily back to earth. It was this rough treatment which had put all but Sergeant Dimmer temporarily out of action. He had been the unlucky one who had got in the way of a small bomb splinter.

They heard the cookhouse plate being rattled again to call the night men to a meal. George would have liked another mess-tin of cooked German food, but Lucky shook his head.

"You know the old saying, George. You can take the pitcher to the well too often."

"Nobody's talking about going to a well." George did not try to hide his disappointment. "You said how easy it was to collect the grub, and . . ."

"There are fewer men going to the cookhouse now," Lucky pointed out. "We might be noticed. We're not going. Taff . . . do you think you could man the gun? Load it . . . we might meet somebody. George, are you ready? I'm going to take off the shackles fastening us to the transporter. Then I'll drive the transporter out of this parking spot. Once we are in the road you drive off the ramp and I'll get aboard. You needn't stop to let me on. Just keep the turret top open. Okay?"

"Okay." George turned to his engines while Taffy looked at the pyramid of shells by his side. While they had been getting ready for this break-out there had been no time to think of what might happen. Now there was time, and Taffy was worried. He shot a quick glance at Sergeant Dimmer.

Dimmer had insisted it was a lunatic move, and that they could not hope to get away. Taffy wondered if he would soon be proved right.

There was a bang on the turret top. Lucky Jordan had unshackled the tank. Now he was going to start the transporter's power engine.

"Don't worry." It was Sergeant Dimmer, who had guessed what Taffy was thinking about. "Jordan has picked the right time. With practically every man on the station either asleep or feeding, you'll never get a better chance."

"Oh, I know," Taffy said, and forcing a smile said: "I wasn't worrying . . . only wondering if George would get the engines started."

He got his answer within seconds. First one and then the other engine came to thunderous life. Then they felt movement. Lucky Jordan had started the tank transporter. He had to pull out of the ranks in order to give them a clear run out of the big tank park.

It had seemed the kind of thing which would not be too difficult, but Lucky had no lights to help him. Finally he decided to take a chance and switch on the transporter's powerful headlamps. Within seconds there was a warning shout from the sentry on guard at the desert end of the park. He was yelling for the lights to be switched off at once.

Sweating as he struggled with the big wheel, Lucky Jordan edged the cumbersome transporter out of the ruck, and into the clearway. The German guard, now running and bellowing angrily, was drawing nearer.

Dropping his foot even harder on the accelerator, Lucky swung the big machine round with a final rush and straightened it up. He slipped the gear lever into neutral and switched off the engine just as the angry German arrived.

"You mad fool," the guard screeched as he jumped up on to the running board and reached across to switch off the headlights.

Then Lucky hit him. It was not really hard enough, though it tumbled the man off the running board.

Dragging out his automatic the German leaped up on to the running board again, but this time the driver's seat was empty. Lucky had scrambled out on the opposite side and was running to board *Mae West*, which was now beginning to trundle down the ramp. The guard raced round the front of the transporter in a furious temper.

Crack! The pistol spat fire. The German had not really aimed at Lucky, firing more as a warning than anything else. For the moment he was not sure whether he was dealing with some idiot who had got hold of more drink than he could hold, or a fool who had become sun crazy.

" Stop!" he roared as he saw a shadowy figure leap on to the moving tank. He fired again. Then, as he saw Lucky scramble on to the tank, disappear down the turret top and drag down the splinter-proof cover, he bellowed a warning to the other sentry to block the way.

Inside the tank Lucky came to rest on hands and knees. He lifted his right hand to his mouth and sucked at his skinned knuckles. He had not hit the German guard with all his power, but he had taken the skin off his knuckles against the man's teeth. Somebody would need to see a dentist fairly soon.

"It sounds as if you've started something," Sergeant Dimmer shouted, as a thunderous "dong" sounded through the tank, suggesting that a bullet, or possibly a small shell, had crashed against their armour plating.

"It looks as if we're going to be stopped before we've got going. I think they're running a lorry across the entrance," George yelled, staring through the driving slits.

"Out of the way, Taff," Lucky ordered. He was the tank's official gunner, and as Taffy slid out of the firing seat, and knelt behind where he could act as loader for the gun, Lucky leaned forward to get a better view through the sighting slits.

The only light was a faint pink glow from the nearby cookhouse, but it did seem as if there was something now blocking their way out. Lucky Jordan never took long to make up his mind. He took quick aim and fired the first round of a battle which was to reach the ears of Rommel within the hour.

They were less than eighty yards from the entrance to the tank repair park, and at such short range Lucky would have kicked himself if he had missed. His shell ripped into the side of the lorry.

Somebody had made a slick move. A wide-awake sentry had jumped into the cab of a big troop carrier, and it was now barring the way completely. Lucky pumped another shell into it, and this time there was a flash from the troop carrier's engine, followed within seconds by the red glow of a fire.

"Do you want to go straight on?" George yelled. He had eased his feet from the accelerator bar, slowing down the speed of the General Grant tank.

"Stop!" Lucky yelled, and swinging his gun round, aimed at the first of six four-thousand gallon petrol bowsers parked side by side some thirty yards from the entrance. His first shell went right through, for the light metal of the petrol tanker could stand up to the armour-piercing shell little better

The shell ripped into the side of the
lorry . . .

than a sheet of tissue paper to a stone from a boy's catapult.

Lucky fired again, but by now he was not the only one firing. The off-duty guards had come tumbling out of their dusty tent, and with Schmeissers, and even a light machine-gun, were beginning to pour a hail of lead at the tank. Inside the British tank the effect was terrible. As bullets by the hundred bounced off the armour, each one striking a vivid spark, the ears of the four Britishers were tortured with the thunderous tattoo.

More and more Germans were rushing for arms, and there could only be one end unless the tank was able to get out. A lucky bullet would find a way in by one of the sighting slits. The gunner and the driver would die, and even if someone took the driver's place he would suffer the same fate. Under such a hail of lead the least cranny in the armour would soon be found by a bullet.

"Reverse . . . reverse," Lucky roared. "Take us back, George."

George flicked his gear-levers. The reverse gear was one part of the tank's mechanism he had not checked. He could not get into reverse gear with his right hand engine, and there was not room for the tank to swing round.

"George," Lucky roared again, firing another round at the petrol bowsers, "Get us back . . . we've got to get back, or they'll finish us."

"I can't," George shouted. "I can't get my reverse left hand gear. We'll have to go on."

Lucky Jordan groaned and closed his eyes for a moment. Seconds earlier he had fired another round into the petrol bowsers, and this time the effect had been instantaneous and as dramatic as anyone could have wished. As petrol gushed out of the first tanker he had holed, his second shell crashed into an engine casing. With terrifying suddenness the petrol caught fire.

The hail of bullets ceased at once as soldiers, mechanics, technicians, clerks and cooks raced for cover. Only a mad fool would have done otherwise, for around the bowsers, and spreading across the road, adding a further barrier to the way out for the British tank, was a flaming tide of petrol.

"Cor, strike a light!" Taffy gasped.

"Strike a light!" George muttered, and now that the firing had ceased and the tank engines were only idling, the silence seemed like that of a cathedral in the dead of night. "What the flippin' heck do you want a light for? We've got too much light already out there. Lucky, for the love of mike, what're we going to do now. We're in the soup, up to the ears."

Lucky peered through the firing slits and for the time being even his ready tongue was stilled. Red and yellow flames were like a wall ahead of them, and the fire was spreading. In such heat it would not be long before the other petrol bowsers burst. Then the fire would be like a small hell on earth.

"Still want to be a sergeant?" the voice was that of Sergeant Alfie Dimmer, and he was addressing Lucky Jordan.

4. Desert Rats in a trap

"I NEED A CIG!" Lucky admitted, fumbling in the breast pocket of his shirt for his crumpled packet of cigarettes.

"You need a sergeant," Alfie told him. "Help me up into the turret, and give me the earphones and mike. I'll take my stripes back, Lucky, if you're prepared to take a chance."

It was a relief to Lucky, Taffy and George to have their sergeant take command again, even if the situation did appear hopeless. Sergeant Alfie Dimmer always seemed to know the answers. The turret top was thrown back with a screech of metal on metal and Dimmer was heaved up.

He switched on his intercom and said:

"Testing, George, are your hearing me?"

"Loud and clear!" George assured him.

Someone had seen the turret top open, and there came a short burst of Schmeisser fire. The German was off target for the flickering light from the flaming oil tended to distort things. Bullets rattled against the tank, and Taffy cast an apprehensive glance upwards.

"You didn't ought to be up there, Sarge," he warned.

"Straight ahead—and get your feet down," Sergeant Dimmer ordered, and eased himself a little farther down in the turret as more bullets began to fly. Then, as the tank lurched into motion Lucky Jordan got his orders. "Fire as fast as you can into the area to the left of the burning tanker, Jordan . . . give 'em the works, or I'll be a dead duck when we get through."

Lucky was glad of the chance to do something. Taffy loaded as he had seldom loaded before, and the gun spat flame almost like a pom-pom. The shells burst among the tanks and armoured cars, shell splinters struck sparks in all directions, and the Germans who had been gathering to pour a withering blast of machine-gun and Schmeisser fire into the tank ducked for cover.

In the driving seat, George sat with his eyes growing rounder and rounder as the tank picked up speed. She was probably doing ten miles an hour when her tracks ran into the first flames. Petrol from the bowser was pouring out. It had soaked into the first inch of the sun-dried ground, and now the very sand, hard-packed under the weight of many scores of tanks, armoured cars, tank transporters and trucks, burned as if it were live coals.

"Shut every *louvre* (sighting slit)," Sergeant Dimmer yelled, and fell down into the tank, managing to drag the turret top into place as he did so. Only big George did not obey the sergeant's command. He had to be able to see where he was driving, but the heat was so intense that it seemed to be shrivelling his eyeballs.

Lucky Jordan, seeing the effect which the heat was having on all of them, whipped the top off a jerrycan of water, yelled a warning to George, then emptied half a gallon of water over the big man's shoulders.

It saved them, for big George, tough as hickory though he was, had reached fainting point before the water cascaded over him. It jerked him back to his senses. Lucky splashed water over Taffy, and then over Sergeant Dimmer who was lying face down on the hot metal of the tank floor. The last of the water Lucky splashed over himself.

"Hang on!" The hoarse command from George was the first intimation that they were through the barrier. Ahead now was the burning truck. If they could batter their way past that, then the open desert lay before them—and a chance of freedom.

The Grant's engines thundered even more angrily as George's feet pressed the accelerator bar down as far as it would go. Like a maddened hippo the tank lurched on, with George breaking the drive to one track to slow it down and slew the tank round a little until it was right in line for its charge.

Crunch! They struck the blazing lorry against its back wheels. For a few seconds no one quite knew what was happening. There was a clanging and hammering on the metal-work as if a dozen blacksmiths' hammers were beating a devil's tattoo on the Grant, then with a screeching of metal they threw the lorry off.

Taffy scrambled into the turret and lifting the top an inch or so, looked back.

"Cor!" That was all he could say. Seen from outside, the German Repair Unit made a wonderful picture. The second of the petrol bowsers was now hidden in a towering wall of flame. In the fantastic heat it had split a seam, and spewed hundreds and hundreds of gallons of Rommel's precious fuel on to the already roaring fire, sending flames leaping a hundred or more feet into the air.

Taffy ducked down quickly a few seconds later, for there were some soldiers in the camp who had not panicked. Anti-aircraft gunners had deflected the muzzles of their long guns and were firing after the cheeky Britishers. For the moment the shells were screaming overhead, but the farther away the tank went, the easier it would be for the gunners.

To make matters worse a mobile search-light unit had also gone into action and its beam was now probing the fire-lit desert relentlessly.

" Better do a bit of jinking," Taffy yelled, ducking down again from the turret as an anti-aircraft shell screamed past. " They've got a flippin' searchlight on us."

George, his face streaming sweat, swung the big tank this way and that. It was not hard to change direction. All he had to do was to break the drive to each track in turn for a split second. With that track stopped the tank automatically swerved.

"Another two or three minutes," Lucky promised, having taken Taffy's place in the turret. "Keep her going, George, old cock, and we'll be happy." He looked down and called to Taffy. "Taffy—get Alfie sitting up. Pour some water over him. He must have taken another knock, or something."

Several times in the next minute Lucky hurriedly ducked into the turret and let the top clang down as a shell burst too close for comfort. The anti-aircraft gunners were getting the range, and with the tank still held squarely in the beam of the searchlight, the only thing George could do was zig-zag.

Twice the tank rocked as shells burst so near that splinters crashed against the armoured-plating. Then, after turning left for another zig-zag, the tank continued to turn. Only in a very short circle.

"What are you playing at?" Lucky roared, ducking down for a moment to see if George was hurt. A few seconds earlier there had been a thunderous "clang" against the side of the tank as another shell burst close.

Almost as Lucky spoke the thunder of the tank engines died down, and George heaved himself out of his seat.

"We've lost a track," he yelled, "out of the way, Lucky, while I have a look."

"You stay where you are," Lucky yelled back, and flinging the turret top right over, scrambled out. They were about three quarters of a mile from the German Repair Unit, and even at this distance the glow from the roaring flames cast a pink light over the scene.

Lucky did not need to get out of the tank to discover whether George's fears were justified. Away to the left, looking like a long black snake, was their left hand track. Either a lucky hit had broken it, or it had been weakened when they had been dive-bombed, and the turning first one way and then the other had completed the damage.

"Well, that's torn it good and proper," Lucky murmured, and slid down into the tank as another anti-aircraft shell whined overhead, to burst in the air a good fifty yards farther on. "Sarge, we'll have . . ."

and there Lucky stopped, for Taffy had managed to turn Sergeant Dimmer over, and having eased him into a sitting position, was trying to get Alfie to take a drink.

"Look, we'll have to get out of here quick," Lucky said. "That lot have got the range, and if they land one on top . . . we've had it. Look at all this petrol. Come on, we've got to blow, now."

"Talk sense!" This retort came from little Taffy. "The sarge can't. He must have hurt himself again when he fell out of the turret. He's fainted, or something. If . . ."

"I'll be all right in a minute." Sergeant Alfie Dimmer was groping his way back to consciousness. He shook his head, screwed up his eyes as if in sudden pain, then with a great effort said quietly: "Look, lads, Lucky is right. You've got to get out of here. Get out and wait. I'll be with you in a . . ."

Crunch! A shell must have driven into the desert no more than a yard or so away, for the tank rocked under the explosion. All four instinctively ducked and closed their eyes.

"See what I mean?" Dimmer seemed to

be more himself again now. "Get out . . . scatter and I'll join you . . ."

"Up you go, Taff," George said, and grabbing the little Welshman he heaved him up into the turret.

"I'm not leaving . . ." That was as far as Taffy was allowed to get. George was a big man, and he was strong. He fairly shot Taffy up, wincing as one of the Welshman's hob-nailed boots struck him a glancing blow on the temple.

Two more explosions outside testified to the growing accuracy of the German ack-ack gunners' fire. They were ranging well, and getting closer to the target.

"Okay, George, I'll stay with him," Lucky said.

"Out!" George said threateningly. In normal times George was a quiet, gentle sort, but when he was roused he was like a mad bull. The bellowed command "Out" sounded as if it came from a bull, now, as it rang through the confines of the tank.

Lucky scrambled up the turret, ducked for an instant, then threw himself out of the tank. As he hit the ground it seemed as if the world had suddenly come to an end.

There was a frightening "Crump", and a shattering scream of riven metal.

One German gunlayer had proved his skill. He had got a direct hit on the General Grant. For a second or so hot metal whistled through the air. None came near Lucky, and he began to run, keeping in a half-crouch as if afraid that the unseen gunners might send him a shell all for himself.

A sudden glow from behind made him drop flat, and he looked over his shoulder. He closed his eyes and winced. That lucky shot had driven through the armour protecting the General Grant's engines, and exploding there, had either fired the fuel tanks, or fired the hundred or more gallons of petrol in the tank itself.

"Lucky!" the wail came from Taffy, crouching in a dip no more than twenty yards away. He had seen Lucky leave the tank and run. "This way . . . this way."

Lucky was shaking. The bravest can be forgiven in moments of such danger, and Lucky was cold inside at his narrow escape. He rose and made a frantic dash in the direction of the voice. Flinging himself face down by Taffy's side he lay panting, and shaking. Hammering through his brain was the thought of what would have happened if George had not forced him to leave the tank. The very thought of what was happening inside the General Grant at this moment made his inside curl up in horror.

Yet within a minute he was swearing, for out of the flame-lit night came the massive figure of big George. He fell into the little hollow, and dropped something heavy on Lucky. It was only when Lucky realised that the "something" was Sergeant Alfie Dimmer that his bad language suddenly stopped.

"You got him out," he said, and in the red light from the fiercely burning tank his face showed his blank amazement. "I . . . I . . . I don't see how you could."

"Nah!" George was sucking a finger he had caught on the lip of the turret, taking a strip of skin off in the process. "Nah, I didn't get him out, you twirp. What's the matter with you? Are your eyes bad? Course I got him out. You didn't think I was going to leave him did you. We're not all like you, Lucky," and his laugh took the sting out of his words.

"I wasn't going to leave . . ." Lucky began, but was interrupted by a move from their sergeant. Dimmer was struggling to sit up. Immediately his three men ceased arguing.

He accepted a half-cigarette from Taffy, and a light from Lucky Jordan, who held his lighter well down so that there was no possibility of the little flash being seen. Big George laughed scornfully at the precaution.

"Nobody's going to see a thing like a lighter while this bonfire's blazing, Lucky."

"Shut up," this from Dimmer. "You're like a couple of kids arguing. How far are we from the Jerry camp?" He eased himself round to try to see the German camp, but the furious fire blazing in the General Grant tank made it impossible. The gallons and gallons of petrol which had been stolen and taken to the tank in the hope that it would help them back to the British lines, were now turning pink the metal-work of the tank. No tank had ever blazed more furiously, and the blaze prevented them seeing beyond it.

George thought they must be a mile, maybe more from the camp.

"Then listen to me, lads," Dimmer said. "You'd better get going. Now don't start arguing. I should have insisted earlier on when I handed over to you, Jordan. I know I can't walk, and I know you can't carry me. Jerry will have search parties out at first light . . . in case there are any survivors," and he nodded towards their burning tank. "They'll see me off to base, and a hospital. So I'll be all right. Now, you three have got to get cracking. If you don't, they'll have you behind wire. Thanks for the fag, Taff. If I ever see you in Civvy street when this lot's over—I'll buy you a big cigar."

He held out his hand to George.

"Thanks, George. I never did fancy being fried—and I would have been, but for you. If there'd been somebody here to see you do it I reckon you'd have got a medal." They shook hands. Then Dimmer held out his hand to Lucky Jordan, and there was a grin on his dirt-smeared face as he said: "If you stick by them, Lucky, they'll be all right. They didn't nickname you 'lucky' for nothing. Maybe you'd better take my pay-book . . . I have a few weeks' money to draw. You could send it home to the wife." And feeling inside his shirt he brought out his pay-book and handed it over.

Then, as no one said anything, Sergeant Dimmer went on:

"Well, don't dally, lads. So long and the best of luck. I'm near enough to the tank to attract attention when Jerry comes to see what's left."

There was a long silence, then Taffy said:

"Okay, are you fellows coming? We'd best get as far away as we can before morning. It'll be too hot to walk when the sun comes up." He rose, clapped a hand on Sergeant Dimmer's shoulder, then walked a couple of paces before looking back to ask: "Are you blokes coming, or not?"

"Yep," George said. "Don't go too fast," and bending down, he lifted Sergeant Alfie Dimmer with one powerful heave, slipped him across his shoulder in a fireman's lift grip, and started off after Taffy.

5. No water!

SERGEANT DIMMER was weak, and in pain, but he managed to struggle so hard for a minute or so that even George was forced to halt. He laid Dimmer down, and before the breathless sergeant could say anything George got in first with:

"Now, look, Alfie, let's have no more flippin' monkey business. I don't care what Taffy says, or Lucky for that matter. I'm not leavin' you. Now that's flat, and don't argue," he bellowed as Dimmer opened his mouth. Turning to Taffy who had come back and was standing staring, big George went on: "And as for you, if you want to go . . . get going. Walk . . . run, if you want. I'm not comin'. Not without Alfie."

"I wasn't walking nowhere," Taffy said angrily. "Only far enough away for us to talk. It ain't no use startin' to walk any-where, not without water, and we haven't got a drop. Trouble with you, George, is you haven't got the brains you were born with. I gave Lucky a wink, meaning we'd walk

Hoisting him over his shoulder, George started off . . .

away an' chew this thing over. I gave you a wink and all you did was look at me as if I've gone barmy. Nobody's thinkin' of leaving the sarge."

"You're all leaving," Dimmer said weakly. "It's an order."

"You shut up," Taffy snapped, and then lifted a hand to his mouth as if he realised he had committed an unforgivable sin. He hurried to apologise. "Sorry, Sarge, didn't mean to be rude—but we just haven't got time to listen to you. We've made up our minds . . . we're not leaving you. If one goes in the P.O.W. pen, we all go. That's right, isn't it?" and he turned to Lucky as if daring him not to agree.

They held their little meeting, and there was some argument when Lucky insisted that they strike west—towards the German bases. He argued that the Germans would certainly be out looking for them when daylight came, and they would expect the Britishers to strike east—towards the British lines. As usual Lucky got his way.

By dawn they had managed to carry Sergeant Alfie Dimmer four miles westwards. As the morning wore on heat and weariness forced them to call a halt. To hide themselves they dug with their knives in the desert sand and managed to rake out a slit trench. Once in the trench they were invisible from the ground, but when a Ghiblin, an Italian two-engined all-purpose plane passed overhead searching for them, they had to cover themselves completely with sand.

Sergeant Dimmer was the worst off, for his wound, as wounds always do, gave him a terrible thirst. By the time the sun slipped out of sight Dimmer was babbling deliriously. His three friends were glum-faced, for they were thirsty to the point where their tongues were beginning to swell.

"If I thought it would save Sarge, I'd be ready to give myself up," Taffy pointed out.

"In that case, stop thinking," Lucky croaked. "I'm going for water . . . and I'll get some if I have to squeeze it with my own hands out of some Jerry or Eytie. You'll stay here and look after Alfie. Me and George won't be long. Well, we'll be back before morning at least."

"Suppose George stays. I've got my revolver, and . . ." Taffy protested.

"Then I'll have it," Lucky said, holding out his hand. "And don't argue, Taff. Come on, let's be having it."

Reluctantly Taffy handed over his Smith and Wesson. There were still four rounds in it. Before they parted George brought out his last cigarette and they smoked it in turn until the stub was burning Lucky's lips.

"Which way are you going?" Taffy asked.

"There's a Jerry airfield across there," Lucky said, "That's where that Eytie plane came from. This is going to be a bad night for the first Italian we come across. If he can't take us to water, well . . ." and Lucky spat out.

The airfield was six miles to the west, and it was the longest six miles either Britisher had ever walked. The going was bad, but their thirst and hunger were worse. When they reached the airfield they discovered it was protected by a wire fence, six feet high.

The "attack" on the Tank Repair Unit the previous night had put Germans and

Italians on the alert. Suspecting the blowing up of the petrol bowsers and the attempted theft of the British tank to be the work of the Long Range Desert Group, the guards on the perimeter wire of this airfield and other military installations, had been doubled.

Lucky and George were now opposite a spot where a sentry stood with his back to the wire. He was silhouetted by the landing lights which had been switched on to allow an approaching plane to land. He was a well-built man and wore the German coal-scuttle type of helmet. This was unusual in the desert but the Germans were half-expecting an attack and were taking no chances of men being injured by stray shots.

Twenty seconds after the landing lights came on, the air quivered with the thunder of big engines, and a Ju. 52, a German Troop Transport plane, appeared in view. It swept in, but at the very last moment, when its landing wheels were almost touching the ground, the pilot decided he was coming in too fast. There was a danger now of his overshooting.

With a fiendish howl his engines were

given full throttle as the pilot tried desperately to get his plane airborne again. The air shivered with the thunderous noise while great clouds of yellow dust were sucked into the air and hung like a thick fog over everything. For two hours Lucky and George had prowled about outside the wire, waiting for a chance to get into the airfield unseen. This was it!

"Now," Lucky said and darted towards the wire. George followed him. He was a big man, and strong, but only he knew how he found the strength to heave up the second wire while keeping his boot on the bottom one. Those wires had been pulled taut mechanically. They were like a bow-string—but George parted them.

Lucky wriggled under. The sentry had half-turned, his hands up to protect his eyes from the swirling fog. He never knew what hit him. There was a resounding "dong" as the butt of the Smith and Wesson revolver crashed down on his coal-scuttle helmet. The sound went unheard in the fearful roaring of the Junkers's engines. As the German sagged at the knees, Lucky whipped his helmet off and laid the man out with another blow on his now un-protected head.

Clapping the man's steel helmet on his own head, Lucky turned back to the wire to help George through. It was as bad as threading a fine needle with coarse cotton, and both men were sweating profusely before George was finally through. By this time the fog was beginning to thin as the yellow dust settled.

Overhead a second Junkers, which like the first contained reinforcements from Italy for Rommel's Afrika Korps, circled while the first one made another attempt to land. The landing lights below flicked off and on, a signal repeated twice, to let the pilot know that he was to come in again. The Junkers's navigation lights flashed from the darkness a mile distant and the pilot lined up to come in.

It was then that Lucky Jordan's luck seemed to desert him. A German sergeant with a squad of men had started relieving the sentries from wagons at the control end of the airfield. He had been no more than fifty yards from Lucky when the Britisher knocked out his sentry.

Now the German sergeant, his face masked by a handkerchief against the rapidly settling dust, ordered his men to double up. They came on at a trot to relieve the man now lying face down, unconscious and likely to be so for some time to come.

George was wiping dust from his hands as Lucky picked up the sentry's Schmeisser. Then they heard the German sergeant shout a challenge. Of course, when no one answered, he immediately swung his own Schmeisser to the "ready" position and prepared to fire.

He was too late. There was a vicious taca-taca-taca-taca-tac. The hard crackle of firing went unheard in the growing thunder of the Junkers's engines. But as the squad of men melted away into the shadows to escape from the withering fire, the sentry who had just been posted some fifty yards away, saw the flashes of the gun. Immediately he turned for an alarm button on the fence post behind him, and pressed his finger on it.

In the H.Q. caravan at the head of the

airfield the alarm klaxon wailed its mournful notes. The airfield controller, anxiously watching the Junkers as it swept in to the touch down, panicked. They were all so nervous about raids by the Long Range Desert Group, that the moment the alarm klaxon sounded, the controller's hand went out to the landing lights switch, and he pushed it over.

At once the field was plunged into darkness.

The incoming Junkers's pilot was suddenly left with nothing to guide his plane down. For a second or so he was caught between two desires: one to carry on with the landing, the other to give his engines full throttle for the second time and climb back into the air.

He decided to climb, but he had left it too late. His landing wheels touched, the plane bounced, but even the thrust of its three powerful engines could not lift the heavily laden plane off the ground. With the throttle wide-open, the plane's ground speed increased alarmingly. A few seconds later the Junkers 52 crashed into the huddle

The pilot had left it too late ...

of wagons and caravans which housed the control staff of the airfield.

There was a mighty explosion. Within seconds the darkness of the airfield was lit up as flames blossomed about the tangled mass of wreckage where the Junkers and the caravan wagon offices were.

Inside the shattered plane soldiers struggled to free themselves. Each man was heavily laden with full kit and most of them were yelling in terror. Outside, German guards rushed towards the wreck, anxious to help their frightened comrades to get clear before the mounting fury of the fire burned them to death. For the moment, the "enemy attack" was forgotten.

George rose.

"Water, that's what we want," he croaked. "Come on, Lucky."

"Wait, you fool," Lucky ordered, and pressed his friend flat to the ground. Not until the landing field was clear of running figures would Lucky allow George to get up. Then they scurried along by the fence, pausing only for a moment while George grabbed a German steel helmet and a Schmeisser belonging to the wounded men.

Unfortunately for George the helmet was too small. He threw it away disgustedly for there was no time to look around for another one.

As they ran on, they glanced across at the blazing plane. The scene was indescribable. Men with their uniforms on fire were jumping out of the inferno and ground staff were hurriedly beating out the flames. There was a stream of flaming petrol gushing out of one of the Junkers's punctured tanks and pouring over the ground. It added its own light and terror to the scene.

Lucky and George rushed to the hut farthest away from the scene of the disaster. The door was open. Lucky scrambled in, ordering George to stand guard. Red light shining through the windows enabled him to see that this place was no more than sleeping quarters for someone, probably an officer. There was a bunk and a picture of a woman and two children pinned above it. Clothing hung neatly against the end wall, and—ah, Lucky's eyes lit up at sight of it. A jerrycan! It must be water. Nobody would be fool enough to keep a jerrycan of petrol in a small place like this.

Whipping the top off, Lucky sniffed. He lifted the can and in his hurry to test the contents, splashed wine over his face and chest. It was Chianti!

"Better than nothing," Lucky grunted and took another long drink. His dry throat seemed to absorb the wine as blotting paper absorbs ink.

"Any luck?" the question came from the impatient George, who wanted nothing more than to wash the dust from his throat with half a gallon of water. Lucky slapped the top on the jerrycan and rushed for the door. The fire was now even more terrible, and the rescuers were risking their lives to help out of the Junkers the last of the reinforcements. For some there would be no fighting for a long time to come. The petrol burns on their bodies would not heal quickly. For others this war was over.

"Water!" George croaked, grabbing the jerrycan. "I'm just burning up."

"It isn't water," Lucky said, but George was not listening. He tilted the jerrycan and gulped and gulped, the Italian wine dribbling down his chin and on to his dust-coated khaki shirt. When he finally paused for breath his eyes were shining. He turned to Lucky to say: " Cor, it's worth going thirsty to get a drink like this. It's marvellous. We should get some more while we're here. Taffy would love this, *and* Alfie."

Lucky nodded. He was suddenly feeling right on top of the world. What neither of them realised was that the Chianti, gulped down in such quantities on an empty stomach, had made them quite drunk.

" Tell you what," George said, after drinking more of the Chianti, " Let's pay 'em out for burning old *Mae West*. She was one of the best tanks we had. I was sorry to lose her. We should do something about it."

Lucky stood with his back to the hut and stared down the length of the airfield. There was no need for landing lights now, for the flaming wreck of the Junkers 52 was lighting up everything. It showed the lines of German Stuka dive-bombers on one side and Italian Capronis on the other.

" Wish I could fly," Lucky mused. " We could pinch a plane as easy as kiss your hand."

" I think you are drunk, Lucky," George said solemnly. " What we *could* do . . . we could pinch a car. Look at 'em. If we got one of those we could be back in Alex in a couple of days."

"Hm!" Lucky was thinking. He looked at the Schmeisser he carried and wished he had more ammunition for it. Then he nodded. With the Chianti making him feel he could do anything, he turned to George and said:

"We'll take a car. You can drive and I'll shoot up one or two of the Jerry dive-bombers. Gimme your gun." He took George's Schmeisser, and they both walked unsteadily towards the nearest small armoured car. They were in full view of the scores of Germans now trying to cope with the fire; but no one gave them a second glance.

George checked the car. He switched on the ignition, looked at the petrol and winked as he said:

"They're very thorough, the Jerries, Lucky. They don't believe in leaving a car with an empty tank. Are you ready?"

Lucky nodded, and a moment later the car engine came to life. George swung it backwards from its parking spot, then changed from reverse into forward gear and began a run down the airfield which German and Italian ground staff were to remember for a long time.

As soon as George was in second gear Lucky opened up at the nearest Junkers dive-bomber. Sparks sprang to life as the bullets hammered into the engine nacelle; then there was a sudden flash of fire. What had happened neither Britisher ever knew, but the plane disintegrated. It was the luckiest burst of small-arms fire ever. The bomber must have been loaded up ready for a dawn flight.

The little armoured car was wafted sideways as a tremendous rush of air swept across the landing strip. George turned into the skid which had developed, got back on to the runway, and as he did so there was another mighty explosion. A second Junkers had blown up.

"Get your foot down . . . get your foot down," Lucky yelled, and crouching as low as he could, poured a short burst of fire ahead of them. In the general panic, when the troop carrier overshot the runway, most of the ground personnel had hurried up to lend a hand. The guards on the airfield entrance, however, had remained at their posts.

They were out now, and firing at the little armoured car. Bullets bounced off it and screamed away in frightening ricochets. George, huddled behind the wheel, tried to blast the Germans out of the way by driving straight at them, but they were lying flat on the airstrip and firing with the coolness of battle-toughened troops. Inevitably there was a "tung" from somewhere in the front of the car, a staggering jerk, and the armoured car slid to a skidding halt —a tyre had burst!

"Gimme my gun," George growled from his crouched position behind the dashboard.

"You can have it, old cock," Lucky said, "but it's empty. They're both empty."

They ducked down as bullets spanged against the metal-work. Lucky took a quick look round his side of the car and whistled. The Germans were creeping forward. If one of the approaching men had a grenade the whole thing would soon be over. Neither Britisher dared step out of the car. If they tried to surrender, the chances were they would be shot down. In situations like this men did not take chances. It was the old law—shoot first, ask questions afterwards.

"I feel sorry for little Taffy and Alfie," George said. "Pity we won't get back. I'd have loved Taff to have had some of this stuff . . ." and he tapped the jerrycan of Chianti.

Lucky said nothing. He was feeling in his pockets for a handkerchief. Perhaps if they could show a "white flag", they might not be wiped out in the next second or so.

"So long, Lucky." George thrust a hand out. "Been nice knowing you."

Taca-taca-taca-taca-taca!
More bullets spanged against the armoured car's battered body causing long fat sparks to fly off in every direction. To that sound was added the thunder of racing car engines. Lucky and George huddled even lower. They felt vehicles rush by, and the noise of firing seemed to grow even greater. But now no more bullets hammered against their armoured car.

Lucky risked kneeling up. A moment later he was digging a finger into George's back, and saying :

" George, get mobile. I don't know what's happening, but we can get away if we hustle. I . . . don't forget the jerrycan. It's on your side."

Lucky sprang out of the armoured car. What he saw when he had done so was as spectacular as any Guy Fawkes night. All along each side of the runway planes were blazing, and though the night had been brilliantly lit before by the wreckage of the Junkers and the burning H.Q. caravan, it was brighter still now. Flames were shooting a hundred feet into the air.

George followed Lucky in a lumbering run, swinging the jerrycan of Chianti in one hand, the useless Schmeisser automatic in the other. Neither man would have won a race, for they were dog-tired; they had not slept properly for two nights, and had fought a hard battle before that.

As they galloped round the big lorry which was acting as guardroom for the newly installed airfield, the earth seemed to come up and hit them. It was the same for both of them—a sudden brilliant flash of light, then darkness.

From very far away a voice, an English voice, was speaking to Lucky, and something wet kept flapping against his face. He did not mind that, for the wetness was cooling and his head felt as if it was on fire.

When he finally opened his eyes he looked up into the dusty face of a man who was shining a masked torch-beam on to him. Then a sharp, authoritative voice snapped:

"Oh, you are awake, are you. Who are you?"

Lucky wrinkled his brows and half-closed his eyes again. The voice went on:

"Come on, quick. I want to know who you are. You're carrying a British pay-book. Speak!" And then the man rattled off a phrase in German, followed almost at once by a phrase in Italian.

"Oh, cheese it," Lucky groaned, lifting a hand to his head. "What happened? Where am I?"

"He's British all right," he heard a voice say. "What about the other fellow? Is he coming round?"

"What happened? Where am I?"

"The big fellow, sir? No, it'll be a bit yet before he comes round. Corporal Hacket gave him a real fourpenny one. He went down like a pole-axed bullock."

Lucky shook his head. The big one! That must be George. The mists began to clear from his brain and he tried to sit up. At once the masked torch was turned on him again, and the tart voice began questioning. Lucky spread his hands in an effort to stop the flow of questions.

"That jerrycan, sir," he pleaded. All he could think about now was Sergeant Dimmer, and little Taffy. "Is that all right?"

"What were you doing with that, anyway? It smells like Chianti."

Slowly, painfully, Lucky Jordan collected his wits and told them of the General Grant tank, disabled and left behind after the disastrous Knightsbridge battle. How they had been to the German Tank Repair Unit, and how they had got away.

"We wanted water for Sergeant Dimmer and Taffy, sir," he said. "That's why we went to the airfield. We got in and a sentry saw us just as a plane was coming in to land. I think he tried to give the alarm. He pressed a button on one of the fence posts, and then the lights went out. That was when the plane crashed."

The officer in command of the Long Range Desert Group whose cars had raced on to the airfield to clean up what Lucky and George had started, suddenly began to laugh.

"It's better to be born lucky than rich," he murmured. "You know, Charteris, I've got a feeling that if we had attacked the airfield before these two bright lads got on it, we might have received a warm reception. Give him a drink."

Lucky was given a drink—of water. Then, an hour before dawn, he guided one of the faster vehicles across the desert to where Sergeant Dimmer and little Taffy were still waiting.

Sergeant Dimmer was almost at his last gasp, but a drink of water saved him. Then, with the sun just turning the grey desert to gold again the car was turned south in a dash to rejoin the rest of the Long Range Desert Group patrol.

George had stayed with the main party

to nurse a lump half the size of a duck-egg on the top of his head. His first question was about Lucky Jordan.

"Where is he? Where's Lucky?" he asked, stroking his lump with one hand.

"Who's Lucky, chum?" a corporal of the Long Range Desert Group asked.

"My mate. There were two of us. We were running from a Jerry airfield when—I dunno, something happened."

The corporal grinned.

"Yeah, something did happen, chum," he agreed. "We had one car outside the airfield in case anything went wrong. We saw two blokes running towards us, one of 'em carrying a jerrycan. We could have shot you both, y'know."

"What did you do?" George asked glumly.

"We gave you the old one-two, with revolver butts," the corporal said. "Only the other bloke was wearing a Jerry helmet . . . so he was lucky."

George looked up, frowning.

"Aye, that's him. That'd be Lucky." He shook his head wearily. "Cor, strike a light! You said he was lucky. Well, they call him Lucky. That bloke could fall off a flippin' skyscraper and there'd be a lorry passing loaded with feather beds. Where is he now?"

"Well, if that dust is anything to go by," the corporal said, nodding to where a cloud of sand was being kicked up by a speeding car, "he'll be coming back . . . maybe with your other pals. He said you'd left a sergeant and somebody called Taffy behind. I suppose with a bit of luck they might find 'em."

"A bit of luck?" George said, and for the first time since he came round there was the hint of a smile on his homely face. "When you have Jordan with you—mate, you've got all the luck in the world. He'll have found 'em."

Twenty minutes later he was shaking hands with Lucky Jordan and Taffy. Sergeant Dimmer was conscious, but too weak to do more than whisper to George.

"Thanks, George . . . I'll buy you that cigar when you come to see me in hospital in Alexandria. In fact, I'm going to buy the three of you cigars."

Ten minutes later the Long Range Desert Group patrol was on its way south, to their base in the oasis of Kufra, and then on to Cairo. There, after reporting in, a sweating clerk turned over the files until he found four names in a ledger headed —*Missing, believed dead*. He crossed out the names, Sergeant Alfred Dimmer, Gunner Jordan, Radio-operator Morris, and Mechanic/driver George Dowling.

"They always post 'em missing too soon," he growled, "mucking up my books."